AuthorHouse™
1663 Liberty Drive
Bloomington, IN 47403
www.authorhouse.com
Phone: 1 (833) 262-8899

Because of the dynamic nature of the Internet, any web addresses or links contained in this
book may have changed since publication and may no longer be valid. The views expressed
in this work are solely those of the author and do not necessarily reflect the views of
the publisher, and the publisher hereby disclaims any responsibility for them.

This is a work of fiction. All of the characters, names, incidents, organizations, and dialogue
in this novel are either the products of the author's imagination or are used fictitiously.

Any people depicted in stock imagery provided by Getty Images are models,
and such images are being used for illustrative purposes only.
Certain stock imagery © Getty Images.

This book is printed on acid-free paper.

ISBN: 978-1-6655-0599-4 (sc)
ISBN: 978-1-6655-0600-7 (e)
ISBN: 978-1-6655-0601-4 (hc)

Library of Congress Control Number: 2020921356

Print information available on the last page.

Published by AuthorHouse 07/27/2021

author HOUSE®

The Wildly Whimsical Tales of Gracie and Sniggles

THE MYSTERY OF THE BLUE GOO

Written by Teressa Hill

2020

To my dear friend Cathie Childers, who took all those late-night calls. You kept me on course along Bumble Bee Lane and helped me through with your zany zingers, laughter, and love. To my friend Gloria Archuleta, whose smarts helped me keep the heart and art in the words you read on these pages. To the whiz that she is, Isabelle Branco-Lo, for helping me educate, create, and orchestrate such a beautiful fun facts section.

To all my friends who stuck around when things got icky and sticky, especially my family and friends who loved me when I was blue and not forgetting the ones who spattered me in goo. I love you too. And to all my family and friends who look down from way, way, way up high in sky, keeping an eye on all the plots, thoughts, and dreams. And to my new friends and to the ones I haven't met yet ...

Thank you!

Most importantly, this series of books would never have been made if it hadn't been for my fur family and my inspirations: Bigsby my sniggles, Gracie my giggles, Annie my snug, and Ozzy & Poppy my nuggets. You taught me so many lessons along the way. I love you!

Thank you too!

Be kind, make a new friend, and you will find that you've been given the greatest gift of all. Your heart will fill with giggles, sniggles, and snuggles.

This is a story about a girl who had red curls and her dog, who wore a hat. This is Gracie and her best friend, Sniggles. Gracie thought it was a pity they were moving out of the city. "I'm going to miss my friends," said Gracie.

Sniggles snuggled up next to her. "It's not the end with old friends just because you move. There are new friends to be had. Please don't be sad. It's not bad; let's be glad. You have me, and I have you."

Gracie gave Sniggles a snug. The situation was frightening and exciting, rolled into one big feeling. So, they decided to make it into an adventure!

When Gracie and Sniggles were all unpacked, they decided to explore. Gracie peered out her bedroom window to see what she could spy. She could see lots of trees to climb, flowers to smell, bugs to catch, and all kinds of curious creatures. A lot was going on. Way out back, she spied a shack. To the beat of drum, Gracie proclaimed, "The adventure has begun!"

Once outside, they saw the place was much bigger than they had figured. Gracie smiled because this place was wild, a jungle of sorts. Curiously, they looked around and heard many new sounds. The birds were chipping and chirping; the bees were busy buzzing.

8

The butterflies were flittering and floating, and fuzzy bunnies were bouncing about. A spider was weaving a web, and the toads were croaking in code. This was just the adventure they were looking for, so Gracie and Sniggles decided to explore some more.

Carefully, they entered the jungle. As the leaves on the trees fluttered, Sniggles shuddered. "Maybe we should have a snack before we are attacked."

Gracie reassured Sniggles, "Don't be scared; we're prepared. Besides, you have me, and I have you."

WhoooOOOooosh!

The sound came from somewhere above, and Sniggles's hat was knocked off. A crotchety voice cackled, "A dog who wears a hat?"
Gracie and Sniggles look around. "Who said that?" asked Gracie.
"Who's asking?" the voice replied.

Gracie and Sniggles looked up high, up toward the sky. Perched on a branch was a big black crow. He was glaring down upon them. "Oh, hello up there!" Gracie called out. "My name is Gracie, and this is Sniggles. What's your name?"

"Bob," the crow replied.

"Nice to meet you, Bob."

This shocked Bob. "It is?" he squawked.

"Yes, it is. Would you like to join us?" Gracie inquired. "We are on an adventure."

The old crow's eyes widened. No one had ever been nice to him. "Who, me?" Bob cleared his throat, "I mean, why yes, of course. I'm always up for an adventure."

"Great! You, me, and Sniggles makes three," Gracie said.

The three began to wander through the brush. Gracie stopped and reached into her knapsack and pulled her magical kaleidoscope to see what she could see. As she peered into it a spectacle of colors collided and then faded. Much to her dismay, way, way, way in the distance she spied something. The old shack had a door. "It's perfect!" she exclaimed. All of a sudden, a long pink tail swung back and forth, like a lazy windshield wiper, right in front of her lens. "I am purrrrrfect," said a voice from above, where a cat sat.

Gracie giggled while Sniggles wiggled and waggled. "A friend!" he sniffed. Gracie looked to see in the tree where the cat would be. She smiled at the kitty, who looked so pretty. "Oh yes, you are perfect!"
The cat, whose name was Lucy, paused from filing her claws. "I am?" she meowed. No one had ever told Lucy she was perfect.
"Yes, you are!" Gracie explained. "No rejection—we all are perfection. Would you like to join us? We are on an adventure."
Lucy was puzzled by this act of kindness. Suspiciously, she probed, "A girl with curls and a dog I spy who wears a tie have now asked me, a cat to join them and their third, who's a bird—why, that's absurd! Everyone knows that cats hate crows, and dogs who wear hats don't like cats!"

Bob interjected, "That's not absurd, that's not what I've heard. Everyone knows that cats like crows and that dogs who wear hats like cats. You should come down and have a chit-chat, like a nice kitty cat."

Lucy pondered the invitation. "I guess I could, it would feel good to be understood." Lucy came down to the ground to join her new friends. Gracie counted. "One, two, three, and now we're four; let's go knock on that door."

Once they arrived at the shack, Gracie knocked on the door—rat-a-tat-tat. "Hellooooo?" she called. She knocked again and again. "Is anyone in?" she muttered. There wasn't a response uttered. Sniggles shuddered.

Gracie turned the doorknob to the shack, and that's when Bob crowed, "Attack! Attack!" Out of nowhere, acorns sprinkled and spattered, and everyone scattered.

"Go away! Quit your yellin'. I don't want what you're sellin'!" Ziggy the squirrel shouted as his fluffy tail switched and twitched.
"We're not sellin', so quit your yellin'!" Bob cawed back.
In a frantic antic, Ziggy threw his last nut. With a hiss, Lucy caught the nut with her mitt, that would've hit poor Bob on the nob.

Ziggy was now zonked. With everything he could muster, he kept on with his bluster of jibber and jabber. He scurried in a flurry, gathering the nuts he had scattered. He zigged and he zagged, picking them up one by one, hurrying to get the job done.

Gracie watched with delight at this sight. After all, he did sprinkle and spatter the nuts he had scattered. Curious, she asked, "So much chatter—what's the matter?"

He slowed his pace, and he looked up at her face. He looked so shattered, because no one had ever asked him what was the matter.

"Silly clown, turn that frown upside down. Don't worry as you scurry in a hurry, my furry little friend. No need to be sad, even though you were bad." Gracie smiled.

"I'll be your chum, don't be glum," Sniggles gave Ziggy a nudge. With a grin, Lucy chimed in. "They'll help gather all that matter that you've scattered." Then she went back to clipping her claws. Bob rolled his eyes because he wasn't surprised. Lucy was a cat who could be a bit of a brat. Everyone except Lucy began picking up the nuts.

Searching for acorns, Sniggles snuffled when he sniffed and sniffled while he whiffed. He stumbled upon Bumble who was settled on a nettle. This wee little bee was not yellow, he could see. This bee was blue and covered in goo.

Sniggles poked and prodded. "Why are you crying? And why are you blue?" Bumble replied, "The queen was so mean because I was blue. I did not match the rest of her crew." He cried and he cried. "Boo-hoo! Boo-hoo!"
Sniggles paused for a moment, this bee was so sad. He couldn't believe the queen was so mad. "This can't be true. She wouldn't let you through with the rest of the crew because you are blue?"
Bumble looked up, his eyes filled with tears. "Yes, it's true. After my day's work, I flew with my crew back to the hive. We waited in queue for her majesty's review. As I grew close, she saw I was blue. I knew I was through. Boo-hoo, Boo-hoo! What am I going to do? Who's going to listen to me? I'm just a wee bee who's blue." Bumble cried and he cried.
Sniggles thought and thought. What could he do to help Bumble get out of the goo that was blue?

18

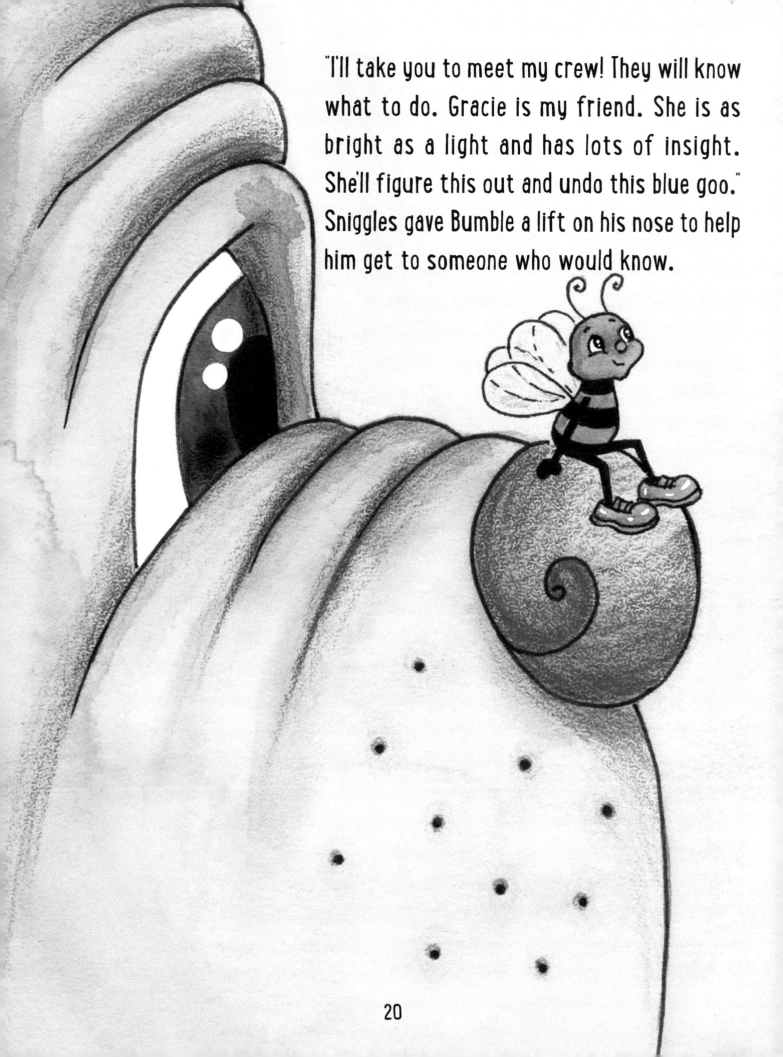

"I'll take you to meet my crew! They will know what to do. Gracie is my friend. She is as bright as a light and has lots of insight. She'll figure this out and undo this blue goo." Sniggles gave Bumble a lift on his nose to help him get to someone who would know.

20

Sniggles waddled and waggled while he whistled a tune. "I'm feeling like a snack, a sn-ackle-lolli-astic-extra-pur-fur-li-cious kind of snack."

Bumble was gollysmacked, "A what?" he asked.

Sniggles giggled. "It's a snunch, a snack before for lunch, or a snupper, a snack before supper. It makes you happy because it's super fantastic, extra crunchy, perfectly prepared, delightfully delicious." He then resumed whistling his tune. Sniggles stopped and paused in his tune, "Hmmm? I do believe it's true. Yes. I am hungry for a snacklelolliasticextrapurfurlicious kind of snack!" Sniggles whistled as he continued on down the path.

By the time Sniggles had finished his tune, he was all the way back to the shack, where Gracie and her friends were having a snack. "A snunch!" Sniggles sniffed.

Gracie looked up, "You silly little snug, give me a hug. Where have you been?" She gave Sniggles a snuggle. Gracie noticed the bug sitting on his snout. "Without a doubt, you made a new friend." She looked to see. "It's a wee little bee, no bigger than a pea! What a beautiful blue." Gracie grinned.

"It's the goo. I'm not blue; I'm yellow." Bumble cried and he cried. "Boo-hoo! Boo-hoo!"

Sniggles set Bumble down on the ground. The wee little bee settled on a petal. His itty-bitty, teeny-weeny knees hung over the rim, he looked so grim. He swung and swayed his little blue shoes, that were covered in goo.

Lucy felt lazy after a snooze and lounged in the tree. She gazed down upon the wee little bee, who was crying like crazy atop a daisy. "I think the bug needs a snug," Lucy purred.

They all gathered round, and Bumble began to tell his tale of the blue goo. "I flew with my crew, buzzing about, until I got tired and my wings gave out. When I came upon a rose, I sensed with my nose. I was tired—it's true—and I needed to tie my shoe. So, I landed on the bloom, then I heard a big boom! The next thing I knew, I was blue." He cried and he cried. "I flew back to the hive. I waited in queue like a good little bee with the rest of the crew. The queen screamed, 'Blueberries are blue; Bluebells and bluebirds are blue. I will not let you through because you are blue! The bees in my hive are yellow, little fellow; now be gone!' she bellowed. My feelers were hurt. I didn't know what to do. I couldn't go home because I was blue. So, I just sat there and cried. Boo-hoo, Boo-hoo!" Bumble wailed.

"Dry your eyes, little Bumble." Sniggles gave him a snuggle.

Gracie replied as she stood by his side, "Your color doesn't matter. We don't see the blue; we see you."
Then Lucy purred, "There is no rejection, we are all perfection."
Ziggy handed Bumble a tissue and said, "Don't worry, little bee, we'll get you home. No need to be sad, you're not alone." Bumble dried his eyes and blew his nose.

"Without a doubt, we'll figure this out! Before you know it, you'll be home in the hive, where you can thrive," Bob crowed.

That's when Gracie leaned in with her quizzing glass to get a closer look at the blue goo. "We don't mean to be prying while you are crying, but we need a clue about this goo," Gracie said. "The blue goo is the first clue. The rose you sensed with your nose, where you tied your shoe, will be our second clue."

Suddenly, Lucy's ears began to twitch in different directions, like a periscope on a submarine. "Shhhhhhh, I detect a noise," she whispered, and she poised herself, her tail flicking and flailing. They all froze and leaned in with an ear to hear.

Boom!

"What was that?" Sniggles jiggled.

Ziggy popped on top of Sniggles head. His tail had doubled in size, he was so surprised. Bob was so discombobulated that he landed on Lucy, who was so startled by the sound that she nearly fell down. Her fur fluffed up, she froze in the air, and she didn't even notice poor Bob in her hair. Bumble's eyes looked hypnotized, he recognized the boom!

Gracie peered into her magical kaleidoscope to see what she could see. Much to her dismay, she spied way, way, way, up high in the sky a blue plume from the big boom. "Look over there," she said, pointing at the plume. "Let's go! It's another clue to the blue goo!"

They all set out toward the big blue cloud floating way up high in the sky.

"I presume we are headed to the plume?" Lucy inquired.

"I assume you weren't listening; of course, we are," Bob replied with a squabble and a squawk.

"Perhaps we should wait to investigate. I don't want to lend any gloom to the boom, and I don't want to assume that we're all doomed, but that's a really big plume," Ziggy jabbered.

"Or maybe we should have a snunch, it's nearly lunch." Sniggles wiggled.

Gracie rallied the crew. "If we solve this mystery, we might make history, all we have to do is follow the clues."

They walked and they talked till they came to a wall. It was a long wooden fence that was very, very tall. "I smell the rose I sensed with my nose!" Bumble buzzed with delight.

They sought to sneak a peek, if they could, through the wood. Gracie spotted a knot in the wood where she could. There she spied Mr. Finkelstein, who was sprinkled and spattered from his head to his toes like a rainbow. He was painting with a gizmo, using a unique technique.

Gracie and her crew were all fizzled, fuzzled, and puzzled. "What's that he's using to paint with?" Ziggy quietly squeaked.

"It's a whatchamacallit," Lucy murmured a purr.

"No, it's a thingamajig," Bob quickly corrected her.

Without warning, there was glitch with the switch, that created a hitch that pitched a boom and created a plume. "That's it!" Gracie exclaimed.

"We need to get in to investigate. Look, there's a gate," Gracie whispered.

Bob knew just what to do. He mumbled his plan. "Does everyone understand?" Together they nodded and bobbled their heads.

Bob left the ground and touched down on a branch way up high to keep an eye on the plot that he thought. Ziggy zigged and zagged up the tall wall. He popped up on top, where he zipped and zoomed from here to there in a bluster of fluster, to distract with his act of jibber and jabber.

"Do you have an itch with that twitch?" Mr. Finkelstein asked. He watched as Ziggy scurried in a flurry. "That's a lot of chitter and chatter," Mr. Finkelstein sputtered.

Without a peep, Lucy leaped to the top of the ledge. Bob was excited. His plot, he thought, was about to hatch. In one swift sweep, Lucy reached the gate and lifted the latch.

"Great, let's go investigate!" Gracie softly said as she led the way.

Once they were in the backyard, like the whizz that she is, Gracie quizzed Mr. Finkelstein. "Excuse me—is that blue goo on your shoe? I'm looking for a clue." Gracie looked around with her quizzing glass. She inspected a bush. "Look! The rose you sensed with your nose, where you tied your shoe—it's blue like you."

Mr. Finkelstein, with surprise in his eyes, exclaimed, "A girl with a squirrel, a dog who wears a hat, a bird with a friend who is a cat, and a bumble who is blue. And you say you are looking for a clue?"

"Yes. You see, the queen was mean because Bumble was blue," Gracie explained.

Mr. Finkelstein said, "My guess is that you were tying your shoe when my gizmo blew, and it showered you in goo."

"That's it! The gizmo caused the boom, which created the plume, which covered Bumble in blue," Gracie said. "Wahoo! Wahoo! We solved the mystery with the clues!"

Ziggy was so happy that he zipped and zoomed and skipped, then he tripped and tipped over a tin, spilling green goo. With his garden hose, Mr. Finkelstein showered the tin of goo, washing away the green until everything looked clean.

"If you can wash away the goo from the flower with just the power of a shower, can we wash away the goo from Bumble too?" Gracie quizzed.

"Why, yes we can." Mr. Finkelstein replied. With a

clickety-CLACK, tickety-**tac**, whackety-**whomp**,

Mr. Finkelstein built an itty-bitty, teeny-weeny thingamabob for Bumble to bathe in.

"What about your shoes?" Lucy asked. "They're still covered in goo."

"I'm going to keep them blue to remind me of you, you, you, you, and you too. You loved me when I was blue and I needed you," Bumble cooed.

"Friends help each other out in times of doubt." Sniggles gave Bumble a nudge.

"You must always remember, no matter whether you are blue or yellow, you are a magnificent fellow!" Gracie chimed in with a grin.

Bob, with a sparkle in his eye, cackled, "I knew we'd figure this out. Before you know it, you'll be home in the hive."

"But I'm a just a wee little bee. I don't know my way back to Honeycomb Hive, I flew with my crew who knew," Bumble cried.

"555 Honeycomb Hive?" Mr. Finkelstein asked. Just like that, he pulled out his magical map. He gave it tap, and it unrolled in a snap. "I know right where that's at. Go down Honeysuckle Way over the bridge. Take a left at Pollinator. Watch out for the alligator. Beware of the hump. Go over the bump. Follow the path on Bumblebee Lane until you come to a shrub shaped like a Great Dane named Dwayne. Beekeepers Inn will be on your right. Swarmy Place should be in sight. Listen for the sound, and you will have found 555 Honeycomb Hive. Then look way up high toward the sky, in a tree the queen will be."

"Got it. Thank you, Mr. Finkelstein," Gracie said, as she squiggled and scratched her notes.

As Mr. Finkelstein let go of his magical map, it quickly snapped back into a roll.

"One, two, three, four, five—let's go look for the hive," Gracie counted.

"What about me?" Bumble mumbled. "Add me to the mix, that makes six."

"My mistake! Let's do it again—one, two, three, four, five, six. Now you're in the mix!" Gracie counted.

Off they went to find the hive. They chuckled all the way down Honeysuckle Way, over the bridge and onto the path, around the hump, and over the bump to Bumblebee Lane. They followed the notes that Gracie wrote until they came to Swarmy Place. Bob took flight way up high in the sky, to see what he could see. Gracie reached deep into her knapsack, and pulled out her compass. She wanted to see if they were headed in the right direction, or if they needed to make a correction and go in a different direction.

45

"What's that humming I hear?" Lucy hissed. They all lent an ear to hear what they could hear.

"We must be near," Gracie replied.
"We're not near—we're here! I know that sound!" Bumble buzzed out.
"Look out! Look out!" Bob blurted out. The sound of a giant crew flying high grew nigh:

Gracie was in luck. She ducked on a dime, just in time. A large swarm of bees buzzed by. Ziggy was so surprised that his tail doubled in size. He popped on top of Sniggles, and wiggled under his hat. Sniggles was mesmerized by all of that. Lucy puffed up because she was afraid. She stuck like tape to Gracie's leg.

"Ouch!" Gracie exclaimed.

"Oh, I apologize." Lucy howled and yowled and removed her claws one by one.

"I advise we would be wise to utilize our eyes," Bob crowed. He perched on a sign, which they all then read, "Warning! Incoming Bees – Honey Hill Landing."

When they arrived at the hive, it made them dizzy to see such a tizzy. All the bees were so busy, keeping the hive heaping in honey. Bumble explained, "All day long, we haul in the pollen. The collectors of the nectar give it to an inspector, who passes the nectar off to a director named Hector, who pours it into jars, where it is stored in a special sector, until it's not runny and it becomes honey."

This made Sniggles very hungry. "Perhaps you might have an ample example of this honey that I could sample?"

All of a sudden, the bees stopped buzzing. Lucy's ears perked up. "Look over there, up in the air!" she said with a hiss.

With a **SWISSSSSSSSSSSSHHHHHHHH**

And a **swooooooOOOOOOOOOOOOOP!**

The Yellow Jacketeers landed for the queen's protection so that she could be received without rejection. Once the coast was clear, her royal bodyguards drew near. The Horrendous Hornets came in strong, making sure nothing went wrong. The Blue Bumble Brigade flew over the parade. The entire hive shouted, "The queen! The queen!" That's when trumpets sounded. Bob and Ziggy were astounded.

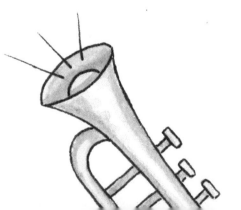

Gracie looked through her magical kaleidoscope to see what she could see. A spectacle of colors collided and then faded. Way up high in the sky she spied, "I see the queen! She doesn't look mean, she's a gorgeous emerald green."

"Green?" Bumble was baffled. As the queen came closer, it was plain to see she was covered in green goo from her head to her shoe. "The queen shouldn't be green!" Bumbled screamed. "She should be yellow!" he bellowed.

"It shouldn't matter her color, blue, green, or tangerine. I find it's best not to be mean." Gracie gently reminded Bumble of what it was like when he was blue from his head to his shoe and how his feelers were hurt by the words the queen bellowed when he was not yellow.

Bumble stared down at his blue shoes. He thought and he thought about the icky and sticky memories the goo brought and about the kindness he had been taught. With a tear in his eye, he thought of the queen and knew what she felt like because she was green. As the queen flew near, instead of cheer, the bees in the hive fled in fear.

By the time she landed, everyone had cleared. Bumble, now humbled, buzzed close to the queen; he couldn't tell if she was mad or sad or just mean.

"I'm green!" the queen screamed. "What am I going to do?" She cried and she cried. "Boo-hoo, Boo-hoo!"

Bumble bowed and presented her with a tissue. "I know how you feel. I was once blue, all covered in goo, as you can see by my shoes," Bumble buzzed.

"But you're just a bumble that was blue. I'm the queen, and now I'm green," she bellowed.

"It doesn't matter what color you are. There should be no rejection, we are all perfection. Blue, green, or tangerine, we all have feelers that are tender. It is love and kindness that we should render. Words can hurt, or words can heal. There is no need to be mean because you are green," Bumble explained. "Now, dry your eyes, we have a surprise."

Behind a screen was Mr. Finkelstein, who had brought along his thingamabob, which would wash the green queen clean.

Once the queen was clean, she was no longer mean. She made a proclamation for a celebration. "From this day forward, all bees are equal. Blue, green, or tangerine—black or white, spotted or striped—we are all alike. We are all perfection and must show each other affection."

Everyone rallied, cheered, and had fun. The celebration had begun. The bee band played a honeybee song.

The queen, in her green shoes, danced the jiggy with Ziggy.

Hector the director dipped his scepter into a pot of honey that was not runny and gave Sniggles an ample sample.

Lucy purred while batting at the bees.

Bob and Mr. Finkelstein discussed how to fix the glitch with the switch that created the hitch that pitched the boom and created the plume.

Sprinkled and splattered in colors aglow from head to toe, like a rainbow, Gracie painted with the gizmo using a unique technique. She colored all the bees' shoes in different hues—pink, purple, blue, green, and tangerine.

The sun started to set, it was the end of the day, and tomorrow was on its way. It was time for them to go. Bumble seemed so sad. Gracie bent down to see the wee little bee, settled on a petal. Bumble's itty-bitty knees hung over the rim, and his teeny-weenie blue shoes swung and they swayed.

"Silly clown, turn that frown upside down. You have found the greatest gift of all."

Bumble looked up at his friends that were gazing down upon him. He wiped a tear from his eye and smiled. "I love you, you, you, you, and you too. Thank you for being my friends. The wind is blowing, I think I need to get going," Bumble buzzed. He waved goodbye as he flew away, up high toward the sky.

THE END

Remember to give the people you meet a smile; it can go a mile and turn a frown upside down. It will come back around. You never know when you'll be low and need a lift. Be a friend and share a smile, it's a gift.

FUN FACTS: The Color of Bees

Western Honey Bee
Yellow
United States

Green Orchid Bee
Blue, Green
Costa Rica

Green Sweat Bee
Green
United States

Giant Bumblebee
Orange
Chile

FUN FACTS: The Color of Bees

Carpenter Bee
Black
Thailand

Cactus Bee
White
United States

Cuckoo Bee
Spotted
Ethiopia

Caupolicana Bee
Striped
Brazil

FUN FACTS: The Color of Bees

Orchid Bee
Purple, Blue, Green
Guyana

Cuckoo Wasp
Blue
United States

Cuckoo Wasp
Purple
United States

Nevada Bumblebee
Yellow and Black
United States

FUN FACTS: The Color of Bees

Neon Cuckoo Bee
Blue and Black
Philippines

Hairy-belted Miner Bee
Yellow
United States

Yellow Carpenter Bee
Yellow
India

Pantaloon Bee
Gold and Striped
United Kingdom

Special thanks to:

Sam Droege, USGS Bee Inventory and Monitoring Lab for providing the pictures

For everything, you could possibly want to know about bees, beekeeping, and honey in one place go to:

schoolofbees.com

School of
BEES

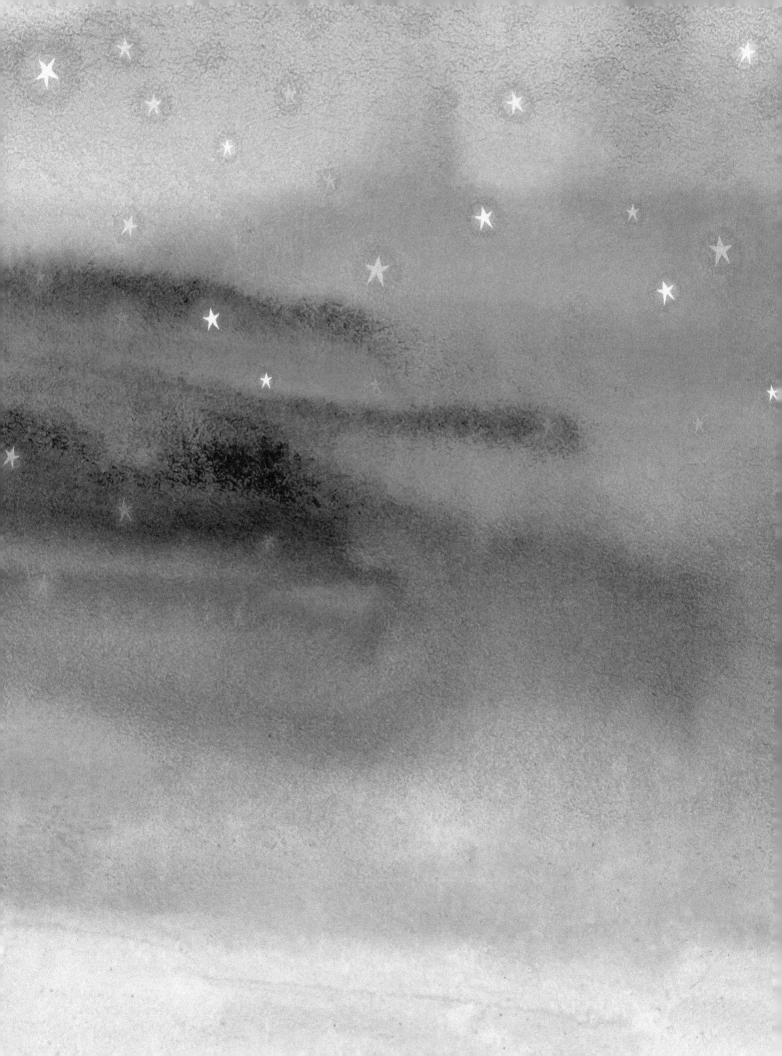